THE MRS. CLAUSE

CAPRICORN COVE SERIES

EVIE MITCHELL

THUNDER THIGHS PUBLISHING

Editor: Nicole Wilson, Evermore Editing

ACKNOWLEDGEMENT OF COUNTRY

I acknowledge the Traditional Custodians of the lands on which I write, the Ngunnawal people, and pay my respect to elders both past and present.

I acknowledge the continued and deep spiritual relationship of the Australian Aboriginal and Torres Strait Islander peoples' to this land, and their unique cultural and spiritual relationships to the land, waters and seas and their rich contribution to society.

Always was, always will be.

To my husband,
there's only one clause in this marriage you need to worry about,
and that's the one that says you're responsible for all spider-related problems.
You take care of that; I'll make the waffles.
Promise.

THE MRS. CLAUSE

Collins

My name is Collins Knight, or at least it was once upon a time. I've been married to Nicholas Del Laurentis for nearly a decade, yet we've spent half that time residing in different houses, different countries, ignoring the reality of our arranged marriage.

That was until I decided I wanted a baby.

Nick won't divorce me, so I'm left with no other option. It's time to invoke the Mrs. Clause of our marriage contract.

Nick

My wife has no idea what she's asking. A baby? Oh, I can help with that. But she's opened the door now, and I'm not about to let her close it again.

This Christmas, it's time to unwrap my favourite gift—one piece of clothing at a time.

Warning: Dearest reader, this arranged marriage novella is filled with jingling bells, unusual uses for candy canes, surprise gifts, and a jolly St Nick who knows how to handle his chimney. So, get thee a Santa Baby and settle in—this sexy holiday romance will leave you hovering under the mistletoe.

AUTHOR NOTE

My Dearest Greedy Reader,

Thank you for choosing to read The Mrs. Clause. I hope you fall in love with Collins and Nick. They were an absolute delight to write, and I adore their second chance romance.

I'd just like to note that the **translations** for this book are at the end of the second Epilogue.

Trigger warnings are listed as follows: Second chance romance, consensual sex, consensual punishment, consensual domination, misunderstanding leading to separation, weight discrimination (referenced), infertility, adoption, dirty talk.

If you have any concerns, please email me at EvieMitchellAuthor@gmail.com

1

Collins

I stood outside the London office of *Knight and Del Laurentis Industries*, shivering in the cold air. I watched the building, my breath misting in front of my face as I hunched my shoulders, hugging my arms around myself, searching for a modicum of warmth. Even dressed in my goose-down coat, wool scarf, and knit hat, I couldn't seem to warm the ice flowing through my veins.

You can do this, Collins. He's only a man. He can only say no.

But that no? It would kill me.

My phone buzzed with incoming texts.

HONEY

You've got this, Collins. Don't
take no for an answer.

ANIKA

If you need me to kill him, let me
know. I'm very handy with a
knife.

ELLA

And I have a husband who owns
multiple boats

BLUE

Between all of us, we'll get the
job done. No worries.

I huffed out a quiet laugh, beyond grateful for the supportive women in my corner.

HONEY

Now get in there!

I straightened my shoulders, sucked in a breath and strode through the revolving glass doors of the imposing building. I'd never set foot in his office before, but the signs positioned next to the elevators indicated my destination was the top floor.

I pressed the elevator button, the doors glided silently shut behind me as I practiced calming techniques. The number above the door silently ticked over as the cart rose, taking me closer to my end goal.

Deep breaths, Collins. Just breathe. He's just a man you used to know.

The elevator doors slid open, and I strode to the reception desk, hoping I projected a confidence I didn't feel.

A man in a stylish suit sat behind the imposing wood and steel counter, one eyebrow cocked as he took me in.

"Can I help you?" His crisp British accent reminded me of just how far I was from home.

Woman up, Collins. You're here to do a job. Now get it done.

"I have an appointment with Mr. Del Laurentis at five o'clock."

The man pursed his lips then typed something into the computer. It beeped and he paled, his gaze shooting back to me.

"Mrs. Del Laurentis, of course. My apologies. I should have recognised you." He stood, gesturing for me to follow him to the waiting area. "Your husband is just in with a client at the moment. They won't be long. Can I take your coat? Would you like a cup of tea or coffee? Perhaps water?"

"No, I'm fine," I told him.

After a brief battle, I allowed him to take my

coat, giving the poor boy something to do instead of hovering awkwardly. I settled on an uncomfortable chair in the waiting room, hands clasped tight in my lap.

The giant diamond on my left hand twinkled. I rarely wore my wedding ring, and not just because it was a clunky thing, always catching on things. I had hidden my marriage from everyone—relegating it to a painful past I had wished to forget. The world of big diamonds and corporate buildings was as far from my every day as could be.

Hence why you came to London.

The trip across the ocean had cost me. My little town of Capricorn Cove in Astipia was a world away from the bustle and hype of London.

But this was where Nick was, and so here I sat—awaiting a husband who I hadn't seen or spoken to in five years.

Oh, I'd seen images of him on newspaper stands or online magazines. Each article singing his praises as the next financial wizard.

A door down the hall opened, and two men walked out. Nick and the man chatted easily, laughing as they walked down to the exit.

My heart clenched as I took him in.

No one looking at him could mistake his

Italian heritage. His dark hair was stylishly windswept, his molasses eyes still brimming with intelligence and unmistakable secrets. Of average height, Nick and I stood nearly eye-to-eye, something I had, once upon a time, enjoyed. But that was before our wedding. Before words were spoken that could never be taken back.

Breathe Collins.

"Great to see you, Erik. I'll be in touch about that boat."

"Of course, Nick. Have a great Christmas."

The men shook hands and clapped each other's backs before Erik, a fellow Astipian if I picked his accent correctly, exited via the lifts.

I watched Nick turn to his receptionist, a smile still on his lips. "Has my wife arrived, Gareth?"

"Yes, sir. She's in the waiting room."

I watched Nick turn, our gazes meeting for the first time in five years.

"Hello, Nick."

We considered each other, him expressionless, me attempting to hide my emotions. From the flush on my face, I suspected I didn't quite manage that feat.

"Shall we?" Nick finally asked, his perusal of me having reached its conclusion. I saw no reaction on his face as to whether or not he approved.

"Yes," I finally said, injecting steel into my voice. I stood, and he placed a hand on the small of my back, guiding me to his office.

The heat of his palm seared through the material of my dress, sending goosebumps racing across my back.

I took a seat, surprised when he sat on the chair beside mine rather than behind his imposing desk. He leaned forward, his hands resting absently on his lap.

I squirmed in my chair, the small of my back continuing to tingle as if landed by his touch.

"What brings you to London, Collins?"

I drew in a breath, knowing this was the moment. "I need your assistance."

He frowned. "And this brought you to London? You know you can call for anything. You're my wife, Collins. You're entitled to everything you want."

Everything except your love.

My heart ached, but I shook it off, pushing those emotions down and locking them away. This was not the time or the place to open Pandora's box.

I pulled my handbag onto my lap and removed one of two envelopes nestled inside. I handed it over, noting my trembling hands.

"I'm afraid this is a request you can't grant over the phone."

He too the envelope, holding it in his lap as he considered me with a long, intense look. Whatever he was searching for, he must have found as he finally moved to open the envelope and pull the papers free.

I'd read them a hundred times on the plane ride over, practically memorising every word. The sheets provided detailed the medical procedure in stunning detail, outlining exactly what to expect and his role. Nick pulled the pamphlet free, opened it, and began reading.

I said nothing. Just sat with my arms wrapped around my handbag, waiting for him to react.

He didn't hurry as he perused the material from front to back, then read it over a second time before placing it in his lap.

"And this is what you want help with?" He cocked an eyebrow in question.

"I can do it without you, but considering we're married—" I trailed off, licking my dry lips.

He watched me for a long moment.

"No."

My heart seized. "No?"

He tapped the papers. "I'm not going to jerk off into a cup so you can get pregnant."

"IVF is a perfectly reasonable way to get pregnant."

"No. That's final, Collins."

Anger, hurt, and disappointment hit me in equal measure. "Okay."

I pulled the second envelope free from my handbag, handing it over. "You've left me no choice, Nick."

He took it, tearing the top free and scanning the document. I saw the exact moment when he found it, the highlighted section of our prenuptial agreement—page 42, Section M, subsections (R) and (S) of the contract.

The clause stated that should we be unable to get pregnant, then either party had the right to either enter into a surrogacy arrangement or seek donor sperm.

Nick glared at me over the paper. "No."

"The clause states—"

"I can read the fucking clause," he snapped, tossing the file on his desk. "I'm not allowing it."

I threw my hands up, exasperated with him and this nonsense marriage we were trapped in.

"I want a baby, Nick. I want a little person to love and raise and care for. If you won't donate sperm, then you've left me only two choices. Either seek a donor, which is within our prenup to do so or seek a divorce."

His full lips pressed into a thin line, deep

furrows cutting into his brow, but he remained silent.

"Your choice." I crossed my arms to keep him from seeing the tremor in my limbs.

Hold it together, Collins. You can do this.

He stood, pacing the room, his hands running through his hair over and over as his long legs ate up the distance between the two walls. After a long moment, he returned to his seat. "We're not doing IVF, and there will be no divorce."

I sighed. "There's no other—"

He held up a hand, cutting me off. "I propose a third option."

It was my turn to raise an eyebrow. I'd agonised over this for months; I hadn't found a third option.

He leaned forward, his hands resting on my knees. A shiver shimmied down my spine, goosebumps breaking out across my skin at his touch. It amazed me that my body could still have such a visceral reaction to his touch when we'd been estranged for so long.

"You want a baby?" Nick's eyes bore into mine, searching for... something. "I'll give you one. But we do it the natural way. You, me, and a bed."

I blinked, stuttering out a stunned response. "Ex-ex-excuse me?"

He nodded, his face deadly serious. "I'll give you a baby. But only if we try sex first."

"Sex between... you and me?" I clarified.

"Yes."

Oh. My. God. Is he serious?

2

Collins

I returned to my hotel room in a daze. Nick had offered to escort me or have a car brought round, but I'd waved him off. I needed the cold evening to shake me out of this shock. It hadn't worked.

You, me, and a bed.

Nick's provocative words ran through my mind on an endless loop.

You, me, and a bed. You, me, and a bed.

I hadn't expected this of him. I'd assumed Nick would grant my wish for IVF or a divorce. After a five-year absence with only the occasional interaction via email or phone, I'd assumed Nick would be happy to scrape me off.

Our marriage was nothing but paper at this point.

But it hadn't always been that way.

I stripped, trying to shake the bittersweet memories of another lifetime. The shower knobs turned easily, and I stepped under the hot spray, focusing on the pinpricks of heat that branded my body.

It worked for a few moments until my skin warmed, and the water flowed in rivulets down my skin, leaving no area untouched.

I'd been engaged in principle since my fourteenth birthday. An arranged marriage to unify Knight Industries and the Del Laurentis Company. I'm not sure if it were mine or Nick's family that suggested it, but either way, the result had been the same—Nick and I had married. Sure, they'd waited an appropriate length of time, but at twenty, I'd ended up believing I'd found my happily ever after.

I'd been sixteen when we'd officially met. He'd been eighteen, cocky, charming, full of the confident charisma that would make him a threat in the board room. I'd fallen under his spell, allowing him to sweep me off my feet and romance me over the years. He'd surprised me with gifts and thoughtful letters. He'd listened to my dreams and encouraged me to pursue them.

Our wedding had been both a nightmare and a dream. It had been my fairytale come true, but with a guest list in the thousands, our parents had used it as an excuse to network. After the wedding, we were to move to London for Nick to work at the new headquarters of *Knight and Del Laurentis Industries*. A new husband, a new country, and my life changing in ways I had no capacity to control.

On the eve of our wedding, I'd text him, a nervous wreck of nerves and fear. Nick hadn't criticised or ignored me; instead, he'd taken the time to help me settle. He'd snuck into my room, holding me all night, whispering that all would be fine once we were married. I'd gone to our marriage bed a virgin, and I assumed he had as well. He'd been gentle, treating me with reverent respect and what I'd naively assumed was love.

You were too innocent to know the difference between lust and love.

It'd taken me a year to discover the truth—Nick didn't love me. He'd spend long hours in the office, skip weekends to remain at work, and meet with clients and colleagues after hours.

Distance had crept into our marriage, passion slowly giving way to indifference.

No, I shouldn't say indifference—nothing

about Nick left me feeling indifferent. Passion had given way to hurt.

I hurt every time my overtures were politely but firmly declines. I hurt after every missed dinner missed, every interrupted conversation, every moment I felt like a second-class citizen in our marriage. The fact this was an arrangement made by our parents only added to the guilt and hurt. I constantly questioned if he loved me, would love me, could love me when realistically, he'd been forced into our marriage.

It had taken me a further three years to get up the courage to leave. Unlike him, I'd been hopelessly in love. I'd naively assumed he would fall for me just as I had done—I just had to give him time and strive to be the perfect wife.

And the gods know I tried. I made myself available to him, learning to cook gourmet dinners and anticipate his needs. I worked overtime, bending myself into knots to make his life easier.

But the words had never come. His actions had never shown anything but a vague interest. With each passing day, I'd felt more like a trophy wife and less like I'd found a man who could love me.

When my sister had announced her engagement, I'd told Nick I was flying over to help.

He'd come for the wedding and had to return to London immediately after. Instead of following, I'd stayed in Astipia determined to start over.

My heart had shattered when he'd made only one attempt to bring me back.

"Are you sure this is what you want, Co?" he'd asked, his voice solemn over the phone line. I'd closed my eyes, conjuring up a picture of him at his office. He'd be wearing a suit, every part of him perfectly pressed. I was certain this phone call would be neatly pencilled in between meetings. A strict thirty minutes allocated to such an important discussion.

"Yes." The word felt like pulling the trigger, an explosion of pain ebbing out from my chest as I pushed it past my lips.

"Your sister's wedding night," he'd rumbled, and I'd tried to suppress the shudder that rolled through my body at the memory. "What was that? A fluke? A goodbye?"

I'd gone all out. Beautiful dress, fancy lingerie, putting all my effort into pleasing him. But it hadn't been enough. I'd reached my limit. He'd left the next morning without even a kiss goodbye.

"I can't pretend anymore, Nicholas. I just don't have it in me."

"You've been pretending?" He sounded shocked, wounded.

I knew it was an act.

"Let's not lie anymore. We've both been pretending. Aren't you tired of it?"

It'd been the last meaningful conversation we'd had. After that, we'd been nothing but distant acquaintances, birthday cards and Christmas presents, and the occasional phone call at a predetermined time. Nothing meaningful, nothing deep.

And yet, my heart still ached after every interaction.

Silly, foolish girl.

I shut the water off and stepped out to wrap myself in a towel. I wished the memories could be as easily wiped away as the water from my skin.

I dressed, crawled into bed and reached for my phone. Tonight, it felt like self-flagellation opening the parenting forum and scrolling through the picture feed. I wanted what these families had, a little one to call my own. Someone to love and adore, someone to raise and encourage. I wanted the sticky fingers and sleepless nights. The kisses and tears.

Hell, I'd become a stalker on the forum. A voyeur watching women's pee stick posts, judging the lines, and celebrating when they were positive. It sounded weird, but it made complete sense once you became part of the parenthood tribe.

Only I wasn't. I floated in the fringes, posting congratulatory comments and lifting those who needed the support. But I had yet to share my journey because it hadn't started.

My phone beeped with an incoming text.

HONEY

He actually said that?

COLLINS

Yeah. And I… I don't know if I'm strong enough to resist.

BLUE

Damn. I don't know what to say. I didn't see this coming.

ANIKA

Oh. We are soooo gonna kill him. I'm looking up flights right now.

ELLA

Wait. What if we're reading this all wrong? What if he is carrying a torch for Collins?

I snorted.

COLLINS

He's not. This is just a way to keep me in line.

HONEY

So call his bluff. Agree to it.

Could I?

The idea teased me as I shut off my phone and returned it to the side table. Settling into the cold hotel bed, I stared up at the ceiling, listening to the muffled traffic outside.

Pregnancies didn't just happen. I knew that. I'd been tracking my fertility for months. And there was no guarantee I'd conceive straight away. Life happened. Infertility happened. Struggles happened. But I hadn't even had the opportunity to try.

You, me, and a bed.

I'd planned to fly to London, convince Nick to be a donor, and then bring him back to Astipia just in time for my appointment late next week. I'd already gone through the process of egg retrieval. All I needed was his sperm.

His sperm. How romantic.

I'd have to cancel the appointment. No point if Nick wasn't prepared to donate.

You could do it without him.

I played the scenario out in my mind. If I did that, he'd have to divorce me, right? The baby wouldn't be his, and there was no way his family would ever allow that indiscretion to go unpunished.

I blew out a long, shaky breath.

Face it, Collins. You'd never do that to him.

I tossed and turned, trying to find a comfortable position. As much as I wanted to be that callous, it just wasn't in my nature. And I would never bring a baby into this world who would one day know they were the reason for so much conflict between our families.

Besides, you'll need the money for their future.

The reality was my job, while fantastic, paid only an average wage. Sure, the benefits were good, but I wanted better than good for my baby. I wanted the best. I wanted to set my little person up for success. Being a single parent would be hard enough without having access to Nick's deep pockets removed. And I'd read every inch of the prenuptial agreement—if I got pregnant without his permission, he'd be well within his rights to take all of my money and property.

I wanted to be a stay-at-home mom for as long as possible. Every woman was different. Every parent was different. I loved my career. Helping people meant a lot to me. But I wanted to be hands-on—and I had the means to do that —so long as I stayed married to Nick.

Sleep evaded me as I played out every scenario I could think of. As the weak dawn light slipped through the gap in my curtains, I finally made a decision.

You, me, and a bed.

3

Nick

I swirled the tumbler of scotch, watching the liquid dance around the glass, absently berating myself.

You're a fool, Nicholas. She's only using you for your sperm. She no longer feels anything for you.

Surprisingly, I didn't have it in me to care.

With some difficulty, I'd cleared my schedule for the next three weeks. It may have been wishful thinking on my part, but if Collins gave me a chance, then I wanted all my focus to be on her.

It had been just under twelve months since I'd last seen my wife. She didn't know that, of course. But every year, when she travelled to Astipia for her annual tax appointment with our joint accountant. I sat in the café in the foyer like some desperate fool, watching with rabid eagerness for a glimpse of her. Some years she walked across the foyer with her head down as she stared at her phone. Others, I was blessed with a few minutes of observation as she paused at the elevators. Once, someone had bumped into, and she'd smiled at them as they apologised.

I'd memorised every second of those stolen minutes. The curve of her waist, the shape of her lips, her walk. I'd greedily consume every detail—the colour of her coat, the number of buttons on her shirt, how her scarf knotted at her neck. I committed every second to memory, knowing these stolen glimpses had to sustain my hunger for another twelve months. Then, after she was safely ensconced in the elevator, heading up to meet with people who wouldn't appreciate the gift of her time, I'd leave, knowing if I stayed even a minute longer, I wouldn't be able to let her go.

And I had to.

I raised the tumbler to my mouth, throwing back the scotch, then poured myself another. The liquid did nothing to calm my frustrations.

Five years ago, Collins had walked out just as I'd been about to land the biggest contract in our company's history. The contract guaranteed our future, preventing the company from imminent collapse and saving thousands of jobs.

But I'd never told her about that. Never told her that her father had misled us about *Knight Industries'* performance. It was only after our marriage that I'd discovered how dire a situation his negligence had put us in. It had taken all my time and effort to pull us out of his hole. Everything I did, I did for us. I'd promised to love and protect Collins, and I'd worked hard to ensure that happened—even if she no longer cared for me.

My cell buzzed, and I leapt for it, a man desperate for answers.

COLLINS

I agree to your terms on one
condition.

The temptation to reply with 'anything' was strong. But I needed to play this out, needed her to trust me.

NICK

And that is?

COLLINS

If it doesn't take the first time,
you agree to IVF.

My fingers hovered above the screen. Could

I put myself through this? Allow myself a taste of heaven only to plunge myself into hell once she left me?

Anything had to be better than the purgatory I lived in right now. This middle ground where nothing felt right, where I couldn't see her, touch her, or taste her.

NICK

Agreed. Be ready at 10 tomorrow morning.

I immediately switched off my phone, tossing it on the coffee table and moved to my large living room windows. I stared at the street below.

If I only had a finite amount of time, then I'd capitalise on every minute spent with her.

I walked to my study, picked up the landline and dialled my second-in-command.

"Bronze? It's Nick. I have something I need to discuss with you."

I WAITED AT THE RESTAURANT, alone but for my bodyguard and a sole waiter. I'd booked out the entire venue. I wanted privacy for this conversation.

When you become a household name, and

your fortune is as big as mine, people will do anything to get a whiff of that money. I'd never told Collins, but she also had a contingent of bodyguards—though I'd place money on the fact she still didn't know.

I waited, sipping the coffee the efficient waiter had placed before me. I'd arrived early, perusing the contract my lawyer had sent around earlier that morning. I paid him an obscene retainer for just this type of immediate attention.

The door to the restaurant opened and Collins stepped through, a gust of cold air following. Her emerald green coat, black knit scarf and cap hid most of her from view. I stood, buttoning my suit jacket and stepped across the restaurant to her side.

"Here, allow me." I helped her shrug out of her coat, tucking her cap and gloves into the coat pocket and draping her scarf over my arm. I handed the pile off to the hovering waiter, who immediately headed for the coatroom.

"Shall we?" I asked, pressing a hand to Collins' back. The warmth of her skin radiated through the thick knit dress she wore, her tights and knee-high boots an additional concession to the cold outside.

She allowed me to direct her to our table. I pulled out her seat, helping her settle, then moved to my own across from her. She looked around, a small frown marring her forehead.

"It's quiet in here."

"By intention," I agreed. "I booked the restaurant out. I wanted us to be alone for this conversation."

Her gaze snapped back to me, her eyebrows lifting in surprise. "Do we need to be alone for this?"

I waved the waiter over, allowing her to take our order before answering Collins question.

"Most business meetings I have are best conducted in privacy. I expect personal arrangements are no different."

Her lips twitched, whether from amusement or some other emotion, I couldn't be sure.

We started with small talk, discussing the weather, her family, my family. Anything that kept her talking as I took my fill of being in the same room with her again.

I knew she was unsettled by the intensity in my gaze by the way her own gaze darted about the room, barely settling on me before bouncing off once more. A flush heated her cheeks, the pink endearingly gorgeous.

I knew she'd be more comfortable if I have her some space, allowed her some semblance of distance. But I could do nothing to temper my reaction. I was like the land during a storm after years of drought—desperate to soak in every drop of her presence.

Our drinks arrived, and I took advantage of the quiet after the waiter left to hand her the envelope. She took it, resting it on the table before her.

"What is it?"

"A custody arrangement." I lifted my cup to my mouth, watching over the rim as her face shifted like quicksand—emotions racing in rapid succession.

"But... what?" she stuttered, hands shaking as she pulled the thick papers free. "I—I don't understand."

"We live on different continents, Co." I used her nickname deliberately, attempting to draw on whatever nostalgic warmth she may hold toward me. "If we're going to bring a child into this relationship, we need to have the custody arrangements sorted."

"But—" She stared at me, her face stricken. "You hate kids."

Her statement shocked a laugh from me.

"Excuse me?"

"You—you said. You hate kids."

"When did I say that?"

"A month or so before I left. I heard you and Dawson speaking about it. You called them nasty things who didn't deserve your time or effort."

I searched my memories, trying to remember when I'd ever—*Oh.*

I barked out a laugh, shaking my head. "Co, I was talking about Joseph Kidd, owner of *Brown and Kidd Transport*. We were in negotiations, and he didn't want to bargain."

My lips curled as I remembered the ruthless satisfaction his downfall had brought. "We lost money on that contract, but I got back at him two years later. We took control of his board, and sent him packing."

Co blinked slowly, biting her lip, uncertainty etched in every line. "I was so sure you meant—"

I gave her time, letting her readjust. The waiter arrived, placed our meals before us, and then discretely left. We ate in silence, Co lost to her thoughts, me watching her with a predator-like interest.

She pushed her plate away, the first to crack our uneasy silence.

"When I came here, I assumed you wouldn't want anything to do with our child." Her words fell like an atomic bomb between us. "I thought we could just—and I'd just—"

I sat back in my seat, feeling her lack of respect for me like a punch to my gut. "You assumed I'd be happy being an absent father."

She shrugged helplessly.

"I may be an absent husband, Collins. But that's by your desire, not mine." I stood abruptly, unable to face her judgment a moment longer. Anger coursed through my veins, igniting a familiar fire—the one that demanded I prove her wrong.

I'm going to crush her objections until I own every part of her.

"Read the contract. If you're still interested, I'll see you at the house at six tonight." I turned on my heel, striding toward the exit.

"Wait!" she called, her chair scraping loudly in the quiet room. I half-turned, shooting her a frosty glare.

"I don't have your address."

I shook my head, turning my back on her. "I haven't moved. I'm still at the Kensington house."

I heard her cough. "But—I thought—"

I accepted my coat from the waiter, pulling it on as I finally looked back at my wife. "Unlike you, that house holds my best memories."

And with that, I left.

4

Collins

Twice now, Nick had thrown me a curveball.

I'd spread the contract across the hotel bed, highlighting and making notes as I read each detailed page.

Nick wanted to be a father. A very hands-on father, if this contract was any indication.

I didn't want to admit it, but the terms were entirely reasonable, though not at all what I expected. I'd made assumptions, clearly unfounded and selfish assumptions, about Nick's priorities.

He wanted shared custody and full access to our child. He was willing to move to Astipia—even to Capricorn Cove—for six months each year. For the other six, he had to be in London and only asked that I visit for four weeks of that time. He'd even compromised and offered to leave London over the Christmas period, which would allow me to take the holiday season off.

He'd built in a negotiation clause and an age-specific timeline to allow for reexamination of the contract conditions when the baby needed to start schooling.

He wanted the right to attend all sporting and academic events, celebrate every birthday, and share all holidays. The contract also held provisions for a trust fund, education, and healthcare.

I could hardly comprehend this new information. Who was this man? I'd been married to Nick for nearly ten years, and I had no idea he was capable of this level of care.

I rolled over, staring at the ceiling, considering my options. Realistically I only had two— return to Astipia to a life alone and childless, or woman up and meet Nick tonight.

For sex. You're going to have sex with your husband.

The thought shouldn't fill me with this much dread.

Or desire....

I tried to squash that dark little voice, but it whispered vivid memories, my skin heating with remembered caresses. Those devious whispers reminded me of a time when I thought Nick loved me, when I gave myself freely and received only pleasure in response.

An ache formed in my core even as my heart protested. Putting aside my feelings, I pushed up from the bed and headed to the bathroom. I took my time showering and shaving, blowing out my curls, and applying a thick but perfect layer of makeup.

Back in the bedroom, I looked at the clothing I had available. Three knit dresses, two pairs of jeans, three warm sweaters, and a lot of functional underwear. Nothing screamed seduction.

I chewed my lips for a brief moment. The stores were open for another hour, and while the dresses weren't exactly sexy if I paired them with the right underwear, they would be a good starting—

Why do you even care?

I sighed, rubbing at my temples with both hands.

It was a good question. I didn't need to be sexy. Nick had agreed to bed me. Hell, it shouldn't matter to me if he needed Viagra or a dark room to get the job done.

But it does. I want him to want me.

And I feared that while tonight may grant

me my heart's desire, it could also end up breaking me in the process.

I made a snap decision, dressing quickly. I headed out to the one lingerie store I knew would welcome me without judgment. The beautiful boutique had silk, lace, and leather decorating their front windows. Wisps of underwear, slips, and corsets were positioned just so within the store.

"Welcome to Sweet Spice," a friendly woman looked up from behind the counter. "Come on in. Can I take your coat or get you a cup of tea? It's quite a day out there."

My mouth moved like a gasping fish, then I shook free of my indecision. "Yes, please. To both."

She helped me out of my coat, hanging it up by the door. "I'll just be a moment with your drink. Feel free to wander about."

She disappeared, and I began to peruse the offerings. I'd been here before, back when I'd been trying to win Nick's love. I'd purchased all kinds of sweet and spicy items— beautiful silk bras in blush pinks and deep jewel tones, lace and leather underwear, corsets and baby dolls, slips, and sexy nightgowns.

I'd left that all behind when I'd run to Astipia. The memories of those beautiful things, the way he'd looked at me in them, hurt too much.

"Here we go," the woman returned with a tray, setting it on the small coffee table in the middle of the room. She gestured for me to sit on the settee across from her. "Let me just get the iPad, and we can talk."

While I settled, she returned, efficiently pouring me a tea and then one for herself. "Now, I'm Mary, and you are—?"

"Collins," I answered, wrapping my hands around the delicate teacup.

"Collins," the woman's crisp British accent was infused with warmth. "Is it a family name?"

I nodded. "For my grandfather." I smiled wryly. "My father expected a boy. His name was to be Collin, but he got only girls, I'm afraid."

Mary smiled. "Would that men knew the value of a daughter." She shook her head. "Now, let's speak of other things. What brings you to my boutique today, Collins? Something for yourself or for someone else?"

I sipped the tea, struggling to find the words. "Well, it's... my husband. Umm, well.... you see—"

Mary chuckled. "You wish for something to tempt him. Perhaps make him fall deeper in love with you?"

I flushed, looking down into the dark tea in

my cup like it held all the answers. "Something like that."

She replaced her cup on the table, settling it just so into the saucer. Mary then picked up the tablet, swiping across the screen and muttering to herself.

"No, not this one. Hmmm, that could work, but the straps aren't quite—ah, yes. I forgot we had that, but the colour isn't quite—ah!"

Finally, she looked up at me, a smile crinkling the corners of her eyes. "I have three items I think may be of interest to you—depending on what you want, of course."

She handed over the tablet, and I took it, swiping through the images. Each of the ensembles would emphasise my curves. Rather than trying to hide my abundance, the lingerie hugged and glided, decorating the model's body beautifully.

The first was a deep red, almost maroon, three-piece made from tulle and silk, a bra, underwear, and waspie corset with optional suspender straps.

"The red will look lovely against your pale skin, but it also comes in a hunter green."

I swiped and immediately decided I'd buy it in both. The red and the green were divine.

"This next option," Mary continued as I

scrolled through the images. "May not be your cup of tea, but I had to add it, just in case."

Yards of skin were visible under dark red leather and shiny silver buckles. The full-body harness was undeniably sexy and vividly reminded me of the two times Nick had tied me up.

My body clenched, a warm wet heat pooling deep in my core.

"The wrist cuffs can be connected to any of the loops," Mary explained, taking a dainty sip of her tea. "I've found that where there is trust between partners, this kind of play can be very enjoyable."

A buried memory of the working holiday we took to Rome resurrected itself, stealing my breath and painting my cheeks with heat.

Nick had come home earlier than expected, his meeting having wrapped up ahead of schedule. I'd been napping on our bed, the apartment dimly lit. I'd woken to Nick climbing up the bed, his hungry mouth pressing kisses to the inside of my thighs, my stomach, and my breasts.

He'd undressed me, and I pulled his belt free, intending to do the same to him. Instead, he'd pinned my hands above my head, using the belt to keep them bound.

"Do you trust me?" he'd asked, his dark eyes dangerously wanting.

"Of course."

I shook off the memory and focused on the reality of my current situation. "Perhaps not today."

Mary inclined her head, no judgment passing across her face.

The last outfit wasn't at all what I expected. While the other two were sexy and passionate, this one was sweet and a little cheeky.

"The holidays are upon us," Mary said with a wink. "Why not give him the best gift he's ever had?"

The outfit wasn't garish or cheap, though it could have easily been so. Instead, the black and red lace felt decadent. The bra didn't clasp, instead, a ribbon tied at the front—which meant that if Nick were to tug it, he'd be opening me as if I were a present to be un-wrapped for his pleasure.

"This and the first two—in both colours, please." I handed the tablet back to her.

She organised for them to be brought from the back in my sizes as I made my way to the changing room. I slipped them on, turning this way and that, trying to imagine Nick's reaction to me.

You, me, and a bed.

Just as I went to hand Mary my card at the

counter, I paused, a secret hope that I dared not feed welling inside me.

"Actually, add the leather as well. And a pair of silk stockings."

Mary grinned, carefully folding my purchases into separate boxes. "Of course."

Back at the hotel, I dressed in the black and red ribbon lingerie. I reached for one of the knit dresses, then paused.

Instead, I slipped on my winter coat and some stockings, with knee-high boots completing my outfit. There was no backing out, no backing down. My outfit, my body, my everything was primed for this moment. Ready for tonight.

Gods help me, I was about to seduce my husband.

Nick

I stood like a villain in the shadow of my windows, watching the street below. I'd been stuck in this position for the last hour, having given up any attempt to pretend that I wasn't on tenterhooks, waiting for Collins' arrival.

If she arrives.

I couldn't entertain the thought. If she weren't here by quarter past, then I would set out to find her. She had come to me, returned with a request I had every intention of fulfilling. She wouldn't leave me as easily this time.

A car pulled up outside the house. It loitered for a moment that seemed to stretch for eternity, then the door opened and a long, curvy leg clad in dark knee-high boots and what looked to be stockings stepped out.

I swallowed as I got my first full glimpse of Collins. Dressed in a knee-length black coat, emerald green scarf, and those fucking boots, her hair fell freely down her back and across her shoulders, tumbling this way and that in the breeze. She paused as the car drove away, looking up at the building she used to call home. From this distance, I had no way of reading her expression.

Was she disappointed? Confused? Were her emotions as turbulent but hopeful as my own?

She disappeared, stepping toward the door. I turned, heading down to the stairs. The doorbell rang, and I heard our housekeeper answer, greeting Collins with over-exuberance.

"Ooch lass, yer a sight for sore eyes, ye are." Mrs. Mackenzie embraced Collins, and I watched from the shadows as Collins flushed at the embrace.

"Ye've left him alone too long, lass," she admonished, still holding her close. "He's been a right ogre since ye left."

I stepped forward, intent on shutting down this line of conversation. "Thank you, Mrs. Mackenzie, that will be all for tonight."

The woman didn't even have the decency to blush.

"Ye wee wife has returned, Nicholas. See that ye don't lose her a second time."

With that advice, she picked up her coat and purse, pressed a final kiss to Collins' cheek, and bustled out of the house.

The door shut behind her with the finality of a tomb. The thick doors muffled the sounds of the street outside and kept the warmth in.

In the silence, I considered Collins. She met my gaze steadily, the flush still rosy on her cheeks.

"Can I take your coat?"

She hesitated for a moment, biting her lip. The red in her cheeks spread, decorating her neck before disappearing under her scarf.

"Okay."

She turned her back on me, her hands going first to the scarf. She unwound it, setting it on the entry table before glancing at me over her shoulder. I raised an eyebrow, half afraid she was about to run.

"It's just a coat, Co." My lips quirked. "Fear not, I'm not about to ravage you in the hall."

She blew out a breath, turning to face away from me once more, muttering something under her breath. I heard the zipper glide down and reached for the back of her coat. As I peeled the thick material away from her body, my cock jumped, thickening to a painful length as Collins's pale skin and glorious curves were revealed.

I dropped the coat on the entry table, unable to walk the few steps away from her to hang it up. She kept her back to me, her breathing shallow and loud in the quiet of the hall.

My palms itched to touch her, to reconnect with her body. I ached to glide my lips over her skin, embedding her unique brand of beauty upon my soul where it belongs.

I reached for her, turning her slowly, gently toward me. Her eyes were wide with nerves and a little fear. She'd laid herself bare for me, and I had no intention of breaking this woman.

I cupped her cheek, stepping close. "You did this." I ran the thumb of my free hand across her breast, caressing the skin that sat just above the ribbon. "For me?"

She bit her lip, bold and dramatic make-up at odds with the vulnerability in her expression. Finally, she nodded.

"Ah, *Cuore mio*, how I've missed you." I didn't give her a chance to respond, closing the inches between us to taste that which I'd coveted for far too long.

Home.

The word burst from my soul, branding every inch of my being with its truth. Collins tasted of warm spice, dark chocolate, and peppermint candy. Her lips were at once familiar and foreign. Her body felt different, rounder, curvier, fuller. She'd grown into her adulthood, no longer the young wife, nubile and girlish. No, this woman in my arms was Botticelli's Venus, arising from the sea, fertile and dressed only in her artful womanly wonder.

My blood sang as I breathed her in, devoured her with single-minded possession. Her hands clenched at my back, fisting my shirt as she made a greedy little sound, straining to get closer.

Without thought, I broke the kiss, boosting her up and walking her the few steps to the entry table. I swept one hand across the top, sending her clothing, a vase, and a decorative knick-knack crashing to the floor.

"Wait, Nick—"

I halted her protests, smothering her words with desperate kisses. For a moment, she tensed beneath my hands; her fists clenching at the front of my shirt, battling between drawing me closer or pushing me away.

I brushed a thumb over the thin silk of her bra, abrading the sensitive nipple below, drawing it to a stiff peak. Collins arched into me, pulling me closer to her. I dropped both hands to her thighs while my mouth found the curve of her neck and nibbled in a way that I knew she adored.

Gently, I pulled her thick thighs open and stepped between them, loving the way she wrapped around me instinctively, her body pliant and responsive.

"Nick...." she breathed, her eyes closed, head tilted to allow me greater access to her neck. "Please...."

My hands roamed back up her body, desperate to memorise every inch. I drank from her skin and tasted her with greedy abandon. She pulled at my shirt, forcing me back a step to allow her to push it up and off, throwing the long-sleeved Henley aside. Collins' beautiful hair fell forward as her lips pressed to my chest, immediately licking and sucking at my skin. I groaned, filling the silent void between us.

My left hand fisted in her curls, holding her mouth to my collarbone as my other hand pulled at the ribbon of her bra, tugging until it slipped free. In one movement, I pulled the bra free, discarding it as her full breasts bounced between us, pressing immediately into my chest.

As loathed as I was to lose her mouth, I needed to see. Needed to feel and watch and taste her glorious breasts. I shifted, bending, moving her back to press into the wall as my hands cupped her, raising her milky skin and blush-coloured nipples to my mouth. The first swipe of my tongue against her had Collins' hips arching, her head falling back, which allowed me greater access.

"Nick, yes," she gasped, fingers tunnelling through my hair and pressing my mouth closer. "Yes!"

I laved at her breast, teasing her nipple, circling, sucking, driving her higher. Memories I only ever allowed myself to remember in the dead of night resurfaced. Collins gasping for more, Collins allowing me to tie her up, Collins in the throes of climax as I grazed my teeth across her nipple.

Every good thing in my life, every good memory, had her at the centre.

"*Nemmeno immagini cosa ho intenzione di farti,*" I told her as I swapped breasts and hands, my mouth needing to brand every part of her.

While one hand stroked her breast, my other dropped to her hip, finding the ties that kept her hidden. I tugged, pulling the ribbon free then swapping to do the same on the other side. Her underwear fell open, and I pulled it away, baring her soft mound to me. Unwilling or perhaps unable to release my attention on her breasts, I instead used my fingers to glide over the sensitive skin of her hip, drifting lower.

"Nick," she purred, still holding my mouth to her breast.

Her hips arched up, searching for my fingers and the release she knows they will provide.

"Tell me what you want," I demanded, pulling back to watch her.

"Touch me."

"Where? Tell me."

Her eyes blinked open; their green depths glazed with passion. I could feel the heat of her, watched as her pulse jumped, her skin darkening with the blush of arousal. I watched her remember exactly what I wanted her to say, watched her remember exactly how wild it drove me, and watched her get off on the knowledge that her next words would send me into a spiral of need.

"My clit," she whispered, a small sexy smile twisting one corner of her lips. "Finger me, Nick."

I growled, surging forward, fingers sliding through her wet heat, my body fitting itself to hers as I pulled her to me, working her clit even as my tongue danced with hers. I swallowed her sounds of pleasure, devouring them as I worked her body.

Mine.

Under me, Collins writhed, a desperate bundle of desire as she soaked my fingers. I remembered everything she liked, my movements making filthy wet sounds as I feasted on her mouth and seared her with my touch.

I wrenched my mouth from hers, pressing my lips to her ear, knowing exactly how hot this would make her. Knowing her ears were a hot point.

"Come for me," I demanded just before I closed my lips over her earlobe.

Liquid heat washed across my fingers as she exploded, her body jolting and arching, locking around me as she came. A garbled scream ripped from her as her body clenched, milking my fingers, her glorious thighs clamping around my waist.

"Yes," I praised, working her clit, driving her orgasm further. "Come on my fingers, baby. Fuck them hard."

She rode me, the scent of her deepening, filling the hall with her perfume. I breathed it in, committing this moment to memory.

If I only have this.

As she came down, I lifted my hand, licking her from my fingers. She watched, wide-eyed and panting, as I savoured her taste.

"Amo il tuo sapore, Tesoro."

Her body shuddered, and I couldn't stop the smirk from pulling at my lips. I gathered her close, pressing my lips to her ear once again.

"You like it when I talk filthy to you, don't you, Collins?"

Her body shivered again, goosebumps prickling across her skin. I grinned, satisfaction burning deep in my gut.

"But you like it better when I speak Italian—*giusto, Tesoro*?"

She pulled my mouth back to hers, her kiss desperate as she squirmed under my hands. I kissed her how she demanded, with hunger and darkness, desperation and desire.

Her hands dropped to my jeans, fumbling blindly with the belt.

I tutted, stilling her hands. "Not yet, Darling. I need to taste you first."

I pressed a final kiss to her swollen mouth and then dropped to my knees. Her thighs clamped around my head as I leaned in, running my tongue across her slit.

"Nick!"

Her gasp had me growling as I continued to taste her, driving my wife wild.

My wife. Mine.

My cock throbbed with unspent need, but I ignored it, focusing on the woman I loved, determined to wring from her pleasure like nothing she had known before.

She came with a groan, her thighs squeezed

my head, her hands clawing at my hair, pressing me to her core.

Don't worry, Tesoro. I have you.

I lapped up the cream, relishing the tangible evidence of her desire.

"Nick...now!" Collins panted, her body shaking with the aftershock of her climax. "Please, Nicholas!"

I surged up, one hand cupping the back of her head, the other reaching down to pull my cock free.

"Call me who I am to you, Wife," I demanded as I fisted my cock.

Her gaze dropped, her lips parting as she took me in.

I, too, was no longer a mere youth. My body had become thicker, harder than the last time we'd been together. And my cock? Yep. Thick and impossibly hard. It had been years since I'd last tasted this woman. Last had her under me. Last thought I may have her again.

And there had never been another. Never would be another.

She lifted her eyes, her cheeks flushed, her lips wet and swollen. "Please, Husband."

I surged in, all control snapping.

Tight. Wet. Hot. Tight.

I slowed, immediately recognising the need to ease myself in. She gasped, squirming under me, simultaneously pulling me in and trying to cast me out.

"More?" I asked, my voice barely more than a growl.

"More!" Collins demanded, trying to force me in.

I worked my cock in her tight little pussy, her channel slowly easing, adjusting to my length. Once satisfied she could take me, I picked up the pace.

"Yes," she moaned as I leaned over her, thrusting hard.

The small entry table slammed against the wall, cracking with each thrust. Collins reached up, bracing her hand against the wall, her breasts bouncing with every violent movement.

"Beautiful," I barked out, her liquid heat surrounding my cock. "You're so fucking beautiful."

Collins reached up, her eyes wild, pulling me down. I leaned in, expecting a kiss. Instead, she moved past my face, teeth digging into my shoulder. I snarled, the bite of pain destroying what little grasp I still had on my control.

"You marking me, Co? You want people to know I'm yours?" I ground into her, pulling gasps and cries from deep in her soul, praying she felt this as much as I did.

"I. Don't. Know," she panted brokenly, her nails digging into my back.

"Yes, you do. Don't lie to me, baby. Claim me."

She thrust herself up, impaling herself on my cock. For one moment, we both hovered together in a way that felt both spiritual and elemental. Then in a clash of limbs, we both broke, crashing together as her body shuddered and clenched under mine, her pussy milking my cock in an erotic massage so incredible I had no chance of prolonging this moment.

I came, painting her insides with my hot cum, relishing the opportunity to be joined with this woman.

My wife.

As we both calmed, our bodies cooling, I felt her start to withdraw.

"Nick, I need to…. Umm, we need to—"

I pulled back, looking down at the woman I loved.

"Come," I entwined our hands together. "Let's get you cleaned up. Then we'll talk."

6

Collins

I stood in the bathroom, staring at myself in the mirror. I pressed palms to my flushed cheeks, my gaze taking in my mussed hair and my swollen lips. A hickey slowly coloured on my collarbone while my butt throbbed, feeling slightly raw.

That's because you let your estranged husband fuck you senseless on a wooden entry table.

I blew out a sigh, closing my eyes and dropping my head. None of this was turning out how I expected. Nick had led me to the bedroom—our bedroom. It looked as if I had only left yesterday. Not a single thing had changed in the five years I'd been gone. Even my clothes, the ones I'd abandoned all those years ago, remained in place.

I'd absently dressed, pulling on clothing that hadn't been worn in years. The clothes were tight but would do until I returned to my hotel. Nick hadn't stayed to explain why he still had my things. He'd simply left me to clean up while he went to make a phone call.

Gathering myself, I pushed away from the vanity, going in search of Nick. As I walked through the house we'd shared, I was struck by the sameness of it all. Nearly every painting, portrait, curtain, or piece of furniture that I'd purchased remained.

Our wedding picture still hung in the hall. The giant vase I'd found in a market in Florence still graced the dining room table. Even the house plants I'd purchased decorated corners and shelves, looking large and healthy.

I'd assumed Nick had wanted me gone. I'd assumed he would have used my leaving as an opportunity to scrub me from his life. Instead, I'd returned to what felt like—a shrine. The only difference between that day and now appeared to be the decorations scattered about the house. Mistletoe and baubles, holly, and candy canes. Mrs. Mackenzie's doing, I was sure.

I found Nicholas in the kitchen, frying something in a pan.

"Hey," he nodded at the seats on the other side of the island. "Take a seat. You want some wine?"

I padded over, settling at the bench. "No, thanks." I patted my stomach. "I'm abstaining from alcohol while trying to—"

The words died on my tongue.

He nodded, turning back to the pan and giving it a quick flick, flipping the pieces of meat sizzling in the pan. "I should have asked you if there's anything you can't eat while we're try-ing." He looked over his shoulder at me, a frown marring his face. "I was just going to finish this risotto, but if you can't eat it, I can—"

"I'm good for the moment," I assured him, feeling touched by his concern. "Once we get pregnant, that's when all the food limitations really kick in."

He nodded, turning back to stir a second pot. When satisfied, he moved to the fridge, pulling out a bottle of soda and handing it over.

I sipped it, watching him navigate the kitchen, adding salt, and preparing our meal. A warmth that had nothing to do with sex and everything to do with this man settled in my chest.

He dished up the meal, handing over a fork and a plate, then settling beside me with his own. We ate in companionable silence, me occasionally stealing glances at him while he stared down at his plate.

"This is really good." I lifted the fork, giving him a smile. "Thank you for making it."

He nodded, but it was distracted as if he were a hundred miles away.

I looked around, searching for a conversation topic to fill the awkward silence that had descended. "You know, you've developed a little bit of an accent since being here. It's subtle but—"

He slammed his fist down on the bench, twisting to pin me with a glare. "Accents? Really, Collins? Five *fucking* years and you want to talk accents? After what we just shared?"

I opened my mouth to say what I didn't know, but he didn't let me, shoving away from the island to pace across the tiled floor.

"Why did you do it, Collins? Why did you leave? You never even gave me that." He turned, his gaze searing. "You owe me that much."

"Because you never loved me," the words came before I had a chance to temper them, and once I started, I had no way of controlling the flow. Years of hurt, of trying to get over this magnificent man and failing, poured from me.

"I heard you, Nick. That night in Scotland with the fucking CEO of *Ridgeway* and his lackey from *Fallington Tech*. Both of them consoling you for being stuck with me." I shoved away from the island, stalking to him, pressing a finger into his chest. "And you didn't defend me. You sat there and said nothing. Nothing!"

"How's your wife?"

"She's well."

"Pity you were forced to marry her. Fat little thing, isn't she?"

"If you'd like the number for some discreet company, let me know."

The hurt and shame, the heartbreaking devastation cut, a soul-deep crater that would never be filled.

"You want to know why I left? Why would I stay with a man who didn't want me?"

"I wanted you," he told me, his face stricken. "I've always fucking wanted you, Collins."

I laughed, the sound brittle and bitter and revealing far too much. "Sure."

"I'm not lying to you. That night? Those fucking bastards? You want to know why I said nothing? Because we were broke. Fucking broke!" He threw his arms out to encompass the room. "All those long fucking nights, all those weekends stuck in the office. The company was going under. We were about to lose the house, the apartment, everything."

He ran his hands through his hair, his eyes boring into me. "I promised I'd take care of you, protect you, ensure you had what you need. Those *fucking* men were one in a long list of assholes I needed to please to ensure our future."

He slammed a fist into his chest. "In here, it burned. It fucking burned to have to sit there and listen to them. To compromise every one of my core values, my beliefs, and my love for you. And I had to do it over and over. Giving time to weasel men, filling my soul with filth until I could turn around and destroy them."

He looked at me, his eyes burning. "You were my light, Co. My one good thing. I'd come home to you, knowing you were safe and happy. You'd kiss me, and I'd feel new. Clean." He shook his head. "But that was all a façade wasn't it, Collins? And yet, even after you left, I strove to please you. To visit retribution upon every single one of those assholes. *Fallington Tech*? *Ridgeway*? We own them, and those assholes are gone."

He scoffed, looking away. "And yet it didn't make a difference, did it? You weren't here."

"We were broke?" I whispered, unsure of where to even start with this new information.

"Completely. Your father hid it. The accountants uncovered the debts nine months into our marriage."

That was about the time Nick had started to spend more time at the office.

All this time, I'd thought...

"Why didn't you tell me?"

"Would it have made a difference?" he asked, running a tired hand across his face.

"Yes." A strangled laugh bubbled up and broke free. "Nicholas, this makes all the difference." I closed the distance between us, placing a hand on his chest. "I could have helped. I could have supported you better. Given you more. Understood why you pulled away. Instead, you let me abandon you because I thought you didn't want me. Could never love me."

"Never," he barked the word, and I felt his conviction. "I love you, Collins. Desperately."

"Then why did you never come?" I started to withdraw, but he caught my hand, holding it over his heart.

"I had nothing to offer you except the threat of bankruptcy."

"But Nick, don't you understand? I don't care about money or things. All I've ever wanted is you." I blinked back tears. "Do you still love me?"

"Fiercely. But when you walked away, perhaps it was pride or self-preservation, but I assumed you didn't love me. And I would never force you to stay in a loveless marriage."

We stared at each other for a long moment, his hand warm over mine, his heart strong under my palm, and nothing but truth in his eyes.

"How did this happen, Nick? How did we get to a point where we've lived separately for so many years?" I sniffed, a deep well of pain morphing into sadness. "We've wasted so much time."

"I didn't trust you enough to confide our troubles. And you didn't trust me enough to tell me your needs." He pulled me closer, wrapping his free arm around me. "We aren't the same people we were. But let's be better. Let's communicate more and work on this."

I nodded, tears falling softly.

"And for the record, we're rich. Ridiculously so." His mouth quirked into what could almost be called a smile. "We're technically billionaires."

I blinked. "Excuse me?"

"I may have sold my soul to begin with, but the tradeoff is that I can now buy small nations." He tilted his head. "Fancy an island for Christmas?"

"No." I raised up on tip-toe, cupping the back of his head. "Just a kiss, thank you."

"Only one?" he asked, lowering his head.

"Only every single one you have to give."

"Mmm," he murmured against my lips. "I can do that."

7

Collins

I woke to find Nick still peacefully slumbering beside me. I watched him with bone-deep contentment warming my insides. I chose not to dwell on the years we'd lost, instead focusing on the now. We were back together, and that was all that mattered.

My stomach growled, interrupting the peaceful moment. I couldn't help but smile at the twinges of protest from muscles that reminded me of all the positions we'd explored the night before.

You know—an arranged marriage isn't meant to be this good.

I padded quietly out of the bedroom, snickering a little as I made my way down to the kitchen, snagging a warm robe from the back of the bedroom door and wrapping it tightly around myself. Humming cheerfully, I assessed Nick's kitchen.

"Bacon and waffles," I muttered, pulling the items out and laying the ingredients on the counter. I found bowls and cutlery in the same drawers in which I'd placed them years before. The waffle maker rested in the same cabinet over the oven, a thin layer of dust covering the lid.

I cleaned it off, setting it to heat as I mixed the batter. Just as I started to pour the first waffle, a loud thud came from above my head.

I frowned, finishing the pour, then shut the lid of the waffle maker, waiting for the waffle to cook. There was another thud, then what sounded like a door slamming. I placed the bowl of batter to the side, reaching for a tea towel and dusting my hands.

What sounded like a stampede of elephants thundered down the stairs, and I saw a flash of skin, dark hair, and long beautiful limbs as Nickran by the kitchen door and headed for the entry.

My heart skipped, and I ran to the hall. "Nick! What's wrong? What's happening?"

He froze, half in, half out of the door, his naked body lit from behind by the weak winter light. A freezing gust of wind blew down the hall toward me.

"Unless there's a fire, close the door," I ordered, wrapping my arms around my middle. "You'll scare the neighbours."

He blinked at me twice, reaching up a hand to scrub across his eyes.

Shit. Did he hit his head?

"Nick?" I stepped into the hall.

"You're still here." He let go of the door, allowing it to swing shut.

I frowned, tilting my head to one side. "Was I meant to be somewhere?"

"I thought you'd—" he broke off, shaking his head.

Realisation slammed into me.

He thought I'd left.

My heart melted, and without thinking, I found myself running down the hall to throw myself at him. He caught me, crushing me to his chest.

"You can't leave," he whispered hoarsely, his voice breaking. "You can't fucking leave me again."

"I won't," I promised, tears blurring my vision. "Never again."

He pushed me back against the wall, my back slamming into the plaster. I barely registered the discomfort as Nick boosted me up, wrapping my generous thighs around his hips.

"Wait, I'm too heavy!" I protested around his deep, soul-changing kisses.

"No. You're. Not," Nick told me between more kisses, grabbing both my hands in his. Opening my mouth to protest again, only moans escaped, my head falling back against the wall as he feasted on my neck, grazing teeth and lips against my overly sensitive skin.

His cock pressed to the juncture of my thighs, my body bowing and opening for him. He pressed me harder against the wall, freeing one of my hands to jerk up the robe, baring my naked pussy to him.

"Good girl," he barked with approval, shifting slightly to press his cock against my core. "Take me, *Tesoro*. Milk my cock."

He fucked me with abandon, hitting me deep and hard, pinning me against the wall in a desperate and dirty move I'd never experienced with him before.

I clawed at his back, words spilling from my mouth with little censure. I praised him, I cursed him, I begged and pleaded and de-manded he fill me with his cock, brand me with his cum, destroy me.

On Nick's hard-edged thrust, I came in a glory of delicious molten heat. The sparks that had been threading their way to my abdomen exploded outwards, lighting every nerve ending until all I could feel was the pleasure-pain of our intense lovemaking.

"Nick!" I gasped his name, knowing it was both a prayer and a praise. He was all I could see and feel. He was my end and my beginning. I couldn't believe I'd let myself think differently for so long.

In this moment, I had no God but him.

He came as I did, in a glory of words and praise. We remained clenched together, our breaths mingling as he pressed our foreheads together.

"I love you, Collins. You are my heart, my soul. Without you, I am nothing. A shell."

I opened my mouth to return his declaration but was rudely interrupted by the shrill screech of a smoke alarm.

"Shit!" I swore, squirming free and racing to the kitchen. "Shit, shit, shit, shit, shit!"

I switched the waffle maker off, snatching at the tea towel and waving it frantically under the ringing smoke alarm, turning my head and coughing as the smoke from the burned waffle wafted around the kitchen.

Nick threw open the French doors that led to our backyard, encouraging the smoke to move outside.

"I'm sorry, I was trying to make you breakfast in bed. I forgot about the waffles and—"

Nick silenced me with a firm kiss, his tongue tangling with mine, tasting of sex and man and the spice that was pure Nick.

"You made me waffles," he murmured against my lips, his body pressing against mine. "I haven't had waffles since you left."

I pulled back, raising my eyebrows in surprise. "Excuse me? You *love* waffles."

He shrugged, not offering a reply and looking a little sheepish. My eyes dropped to his naked form.

"You should go put some clothes on before you get frostbite."

"Never." He pulled me close, lifting me in his strong arms and swinging us around.

I laughed, clutching at his shoulders. "Your hands are freezing!"

"You'll warm me up, won't you, *Tesoro*?"

"No!" I laughed, playfully kicking my legs. "Put me down! I need to make breakfast."

He slid me down his body as if he were reluctant to allow me to escape and ensured I felt every inch of him. He pressed his forehead to mine once again, his eyes turning serious, raw with emotion.

"Grazie per avermi restituito il mio cuore. Senza di te, il mio petto era una cavità vuota, la mia vita

senza luce o speranza. Sei la mia anima, Collins. Il mio tutto."

I melted against him at his declaration of love, offering him my lips. He took them in a sweet kiss filled with promises and hope.

"I love you, Nicholas Del Laurentis. Thank you for waiting for my waffles."

8

Nick

Christmas Eve wasn't turning out at all how I expected. The last two weeks spent with Collins were fucking awesome. The contract was now a moot point. We'd spent our days wandering London's streets and visiting old haunts, rekindling the relationship we always should have had, one conversation at a time. But as soon as darkness fell, we'd spent our nights exploring each other, rediscovering wants and desires. Building trust.

I was in a foul mood, having had an unavoidable last-minute meeting to attend. Collins had waved me off with a smile, but a small part of me had remained fearful that I'd return home to find her gone.

After a very long two hours, I'd opened the door, stomping off the sleet from my boots and shaking out my coat when Collins' husky voice stopped me dead.

"Can I help you with that, Mister Del Laurentis?"

I glanced up, my body freezing in place as I took her in. Dressed in a short red velvet robe trimmed with fake white fur, she wore a sexy smile and thigh-high stockings with heels.

I swallowed a growl as all the blood in my body immediately rushed to my cock.

"And you are?" I asked, playing along.

"Mrs. Claus, of course." She bobbed into a little curtsy, eyes twinkling. "Just here to give you an early Christmas present."

I raised an eyebrow, crossing my arms, amusement and arousal competing for dominance. "And that is?"

With a wicked grin, she dropped the robe, letting it fall to pool around her feet.

Any remaining brain cells I had in my blood-deprived brain immediately imploded.

She wore nothing but the heels and stockings, and a full-body leather harness. The red straps buckled around her thick thighs, her broad hips, and wrapped over and under her gloriously full breasts, lifting them in a way that made my mouth water.

Her nipples had small pasties attached to them, candy canes that jingled with little bells hung from the tips.

"You like?" she asked, placing her hands on her hips and dipping this way and that to show off. The tinkle of the bells drove me wild.

"Come here." I barely recognised the demand as my own.

My body felt like steel, my cock thick and heavy, ready to fuck her, ready to claim this sexy vixen as my own. I wanted to mark her, jerk my cock until I came over her glorious tits, and suck her skin until everyone could see how much I wanted her.

She swayed toward me, Eve tempting Adam to sin, a Madonna ready to give up her virgin Mary title.

"On your knees."

She paused, eyebrows lifting slightly in surprise. I waited, watching her make a decision. She closed the distance between us, helping me remove my coat and hanging it on the hooks in the entry. I watched her walk away from me. Leather wrapped around her waist and hips, straps cutting across both butt cheeks, emphasising the abundance of her curves.

Patience, Nicholas.

It took everything I had to keep my feet planted.

Returning, Collins flicked her head, sending curls bouncing.

"You done?" I asked, injecting boredom I didn't feel into my tone.

She smiled, immediately dropping to her knees and crawling like a panther the last few inches to me.

Think about debt or taxes or your grandmother or—

Collins reached for my pants and, with excruciating slowness, unbuckled my belt, pulling it free in one smooth move.

She hesitated, sliding the leather through her palm and looked up at me shyly. "Do you want to use this on me?"

My cock, already brutally hard, jerked. The memory of that one time I'd lost control briefly invaded my thoughts, using my belt to bind her hands, the explosion of kinky need that had resulted from exploring this one fantasy.

"Give it to me," I told her, holding a hand out.

Her cheeks flushed, her pulse fluttering at her throat. She laid it in my hand, letting me take it and roll it slowly around one of my hands, like a fighter readying himself before a bout.

"I believe I gave you an order, Mrs. Claus."

She blinked, her mouth dropping open. "But I thought—"

I tutted, cutting her off. Leaning down, I grazed the hand wrapped in leather gently across her cheek. "I need your mouth, *Tesoro*."

She shuddered, her body flushing all over. "Yes, sir."

She reached forward, unbuttoning my dress pants and inching my zip down. My cock, turgid and aching, strained against the fabric of my briefs. I waited, allowing her to pull down my pants just far enough to allow her to free my cock.

The bells jingled, and the candy canes swayed on her nipples with her movements. I wanted to reach down and tease those pasties, but I kept still and bided my time. The fact she wore nothing but strips of leather, her glorious skin on display while I remained mostly dressed, added to the heat of the moment. I knew she enjoyed it, revelling in the dichotomy of our situation. My refusal to touch her seemed to add to her pleasure.

Leaning forward, Collins hesitated for one brief moment before fisting the base of my cock as she wrapped her mouth around me.

Hot. Wet. Fucking incredible.

Collins' mouth was everything I remembered and more. She stroked my length with her tongue, flicking playfully at the underside of my crown, pulling curses from me as I stared down at her.

"Fuck. Jesus. Fuck. Christ. Fuck. Yes." I reached down, fisting her long hair, pulling it back to allow me better viewing.

Collins wrapped her lips tight around me, taking me as deep as she could. My eyes rolled back in my head as words spilled from my mouth, praising her, worshipping her, demanding she give me everything.

"Yes, *Tesoro!*" I groaned, encouraging her to suck me deeper, harder. "Take it. Take me. Take everything."

It took every piece of willpower I possessed to stop my hips from thrusting my aching cock down her throat. My body wanted nothing more than to fuck her mouth until all she knew was me.

She drew back, blinking up at me with big eyes. "Nick?"

I forced air into my lungs, panting with desperate desire but needing to ensure she was okay.

"You good, baby?"

She licked her lips, hand still firmly around my cock. "Later, in the bedroom, I want you to spank me."

Fuck.

My control snapped, and I reached down, mindless in my need.

"Suck my cock. I need to cum on your pretty fucking tits."

She moaned, her eyes dropping to half-mast as she shifted forward, her hot little mouth closing around me once more.

She sucked me hard, fisting my cock and deep-throating me with hungry little whimpers.

Fuck. This is my wife. God, I love her.

"You need me, baby?" I asked, my voice rough with need. Her hands crept up, her hips moving higher as she squirmed on the floor. "You like sucking this cock?"

She moaned, her hips shifting restlessly.

"Suck me, baby. Suck this cock."

She took me deep, and I immediately pulled out, splashing her breasts and those fucking candy canes with cum. She whimpered, a sexy little sound of need as I groaned, fisting my cock and jerking it over her breasts, decorating them with my mark.

In the aftermath, we both panted, her flushed and needy, me drained but not anywhere near sated.

I looked down at her, giving my cock one last tug.

"Get in the bedroom."

She pushed up, slightly unsteady but gaining balance as she hurried toward the stairs. I waited, squeezing the belt wrapped around my hand and adjusting my pants, watching her juicy butt jiggling as she disappeared up the stairs.

I waited one more moment before I stalked up the stairs, following her perfume and listening to the sounds of the bells coming from the bedroom.

I found her spread out on the bed, facing the door. Her legs were splayed, fingers playing between her legs as she watched me, that pouty little sex kitten smile playing on her lips.

I stopped in the doorway, leaning my weight on the frame, crossing my arms as I watched her, my cock growing hard at the sight.

"Did I give you permission to touch yourself?" I asked lightly.

Her fingers hesitated, stilling. "No?"

"No," I clarified. "Then what are you doing?"

She bit her lip, her breathing growing faster, her body ready for me. "Getting ready for you."

I suppressed my grin, forcing a frown to appear instead. "Did I ask you to?"

She shook her head.

"What does that mean?"

Her fingers stopped completely, her hand falling away from her body. "I've been naughty."

"Mmm," I hummed, taking a step into the bedroom. "And what happens to naughty girls?"

She blinked slowly, her body moving restlessly. "They're punished."

"Do you need to be punished, Collins?"

"Yes, sir."

"Roll over."

She rolled onto her stomach, and I gently pulled her hands back, using the belt to bind them behind her. Satisfied that the belt was tight enough to keep her hands in place but not tight enough to hurt her too much, I leaned over her, allowing my clothes to drag across her bare skin as my lips found the shell of her ear.

"Gonna spank you now, baby. And you're gonna love it."

She squirmed, a hungry little noise escaping her throat. I grinned, rocking back to sit on the bed, surveying her gorgeous rear. Running hands down her back, I trailed fingers across the globes of her ass, drawing out the moment, letting the anticipation build. I laid a quick tap to her right cheek, the movement designed to startle rather than hurt.

Pain and pleasure were a fine line, and I'd spent years thinking about moments like these, imagining all varieties of scenarios. The reality was so much better than anything I could conceive. Previously, we'd only begun to scratch the surface of this aspect of our relationship. I wasn't about to ruin it by fucking this up.

Under me, Collins squirmed, the sharp tap sending her higher.

"One," she panted, her hips arching.

I gave her another tap, enjoying her groans.

"Two."

Every tap pushed her further, every spank making her wetter until her cream decorated her thighs.

"Please," she begged. "Please, Nick."

As much as I was dying to enter the wet heat of Collins' pussy, I held strong and demanded more.

Another tap.

"Three."

Squirming again, Collins begged, her needy cries killing me.

"One more," I grunted, my hand hovering above her ass. For a breathless moment, we were suspended in a pleasure-pain state of knowing it was about to come, wishing it wouldn't while begging for it to occur.

I tapped her, the smack of her flesh as satisfying as the needy whimper she made as she called, "Four."

Unable to contain myself, I ripped down my pants, tossed off my shirt, and covered her like a rutting bull. I guided my cock to her entrance, teasing us both for a moment, then thrust in. My cock slid through her silky depths, driving us both crazy as she clenched around my hard length with every thrust.

"That's it. Take me, baby. Feel how big I am. This is your cock, *Tesoro*. All yours. Fuck it."

She exploded under me, her hands trapped between us. Her mouth, her fucking mouth, cursed me, praised me, begged me. Instead of easing my pace, I drove us higher, laying hard taps against her ass before running soothing hands over the sting.

Once, twice, three times, and Collins exploded again. She shuddered, her body milking my cock and tipping me over. I came hard, fucking her through both our climaxes, needing to fuck her until we were both spent, needing her to lose all sense of self and yield to me.

We collapsed on the bed, a sweaty, gasping mess of limbs. I rolled us, immediately reaching down to free her hands.

She lay still for a long moment, letting me run comforting hands over her back.

"I think you broke me," she croaked, still not moving. "I actually think my vagina is broken."

I grinned, inordinately pleased with her declaration.

"Don't you grin at me, Nicholas," she barked, still face down.

"Never, wife," I murmured, still running hands over her back. "I live only for your pleasure."

She snorted, rolling to curl into me. "As it should be."

As it always will be. I promise.

9

Collins

I stared down at my underwear with a growing sense of dismay. The first trace of blood lined the inside.

Fighting tears, I cleaned up the mess.

No baby.

I returned to the lounge room, finding Nick slumped across the couch watching Die Hard, a large bowl of popcorn precariously balanced on his stomach.

I sat down, snuggling into his side, trying and failing to stop the tears.

"Hey." He reached over, lifting my head. "What's wrong?"

I sniffed, my eyes drifting to where Bruce

Willis was crawling through air ducts. "Nothing."

"Bullshit." Nick reached out, pausing the movie, shoving the bowl to the side. He turned me fully toward him, giving me his full attention. "Tell me."

I sighed, scrubbing a hand over my face. "I got my period. I know I shouldn't be upset because we just reconnected and the timing is all wrong but—"

"But you wanted our baby." Nick's voice was warm and understanding.

I nodded, still unable to meet his eyes. He gently tilted my head, forcing me to look him in the eye.

"We have time, Collins. All the time in the world. This isn't the end for us. And if we can't conceive, we have adoption. Hell, we can conceive and adopt if you want."

He brushed a thumb across my cheek, swiping away the stray tears. "I'm in this for the long haul, *Tesoro*. You can grieve for this lost moment. But I won't allow you to remain sad. This time together is too precious for that."

My heart beat with the bittersweet knowledge that he was right. "I'm sorry."

He tutted, shaking his head. "Never apologise, *Tesoro*. You are my heart, and when you ache, I ache. You can always feel; always tell me what you feel. There is no judgment in this house."

I sighed, settling into him. We stayed like that for a long moment, enjoying this feeling.

"You need anything?" he asked.

"No," I whispered back, loving the feel of him in my arms. "I just can't believe I'm actually here with you."

"Explain?"

I shrugged. "Life never felt right without you."

He sighed, running fingers through my hair. "I know."

I tilted my head back, raising an eyebrow in question.

"I missed you. Every single day. All I wanted was another moment, one touch." He blew out a breath. "Life felt less without you."

The silence felt easy, even though it was filled with regret.

"What do we do now? Do I move here?" I asked, wondering if I was really ready to move back to London.

"I've been thinking about that." He reached over, pulled his phone off the coffee table and handed it to me. "The Cove isn't ideal for my business, but this house—?"

I looked at the small screen, flicking

through the vendor pictures of the giant house and large parcel of land.

"It has permission for a helicopter. We could live in the Cove for half the year, London the other half. I can commute when I need to, and work from home the rest of the time."

I stared at the phone and then blinked, tears once again burning. "You'd do that for me?"

He chuckled, "*Tesoro*, I'd do anything for you."

His hand slipped down, resting on my belly. "And for any children we have. I want them to enjoy space and sea but also experience the culture clash of a big city."

I sniffled. "I love you."

"I love you too." He tapped the phone. "So, do I put in an offer?"

I looked back down, considering the beautiful home. "Not yet. Let's see it first."

He raised an eyebrow.

"We might be able to negotiate on the price." I grinned. "After all, I wouldn't want you to spend all your billions in one place."

Nick chuckled, his beautiful dark eyes sparkling. "No, we wouldn't want that."

We watched the rest of Die Hard, snuggled together sharing a bowl of popcorn.

"Collins?" he asked as the movie ended.

"Mmm?"

"About those candy cane pasties—"

I grinned. "Yes?"

"Go put them on. I wanna make those bells jingle."

And ho ho ho, Nick did just that.

Merry Christmas to me.

10

Nick

The phone rang, jerking me awake.

"What time is it?" Collins muttered, rolling over and smacking a pillow over her head.

I glanced at the clock, frowning. "After three."

"On New Year's Day? Tell them to go fuck themselves."

I reached for the phone, chuckling as I picked it up. "This better be good."

"Nick?" Collins' brother-in-law sounded shocked. "What the fuck? Where's Collins?"

"Hello to you too, Cal. My wife is here, beside me. In London. In bed."

Collins pulled the pillow down, her eyebrows raised. "Cal? What's he want?"

"Can you put Collins on? Emily's been—" his voice cracked.

"Fuck, what's happened?"

Cal sounded broken. "I don't know. We separated after Thanksgiving. They found her car wrecked by the side of the road. They're not sure how long she was there, but... it's not good. She's not waking up. It's a coma. Fuck, Nick. I—"

"We're on our way. I'll call you from the airport."

"Thanks."

"If anything changes—"

"I'll let you know," Cal promised.

We ended the call, Collins' big eyes staring at me. "Emily?"

"She's been in an accident. She's in a coma." I cupped my girl's face. "We'll take the jet. I'll call the pilot now. I promise *Tesoro*, we'll get there as soon as humanly possible."

A text lit Collins' phone and I handed it over.

HONEY

Babe, Emily's been in a car accident. Cal is losing his mind. We need you home. Now.

Cal was Honey's big brother. It was how they'd met all those years ago at Emily's wedding.

The next hour was a blur as we rushed through our packing, hurrying to the airport where my private jet was being readied.

"Welcome on board, Mr. Del Laurent's, Mrs. Del Laurentis," the hostess greeted. "Please take a seat. We'll begin takeoff in the next few minutes."

Seated, I intertwined our fingers, squeezing Collins' hand. Her skin felt cold, her expression closed.

"Talk to me," I whispered. "Don't close me out."

She turned her head, her big eyes searching my face.

"She's my little sister."

"I know."

"She's been an absolute bitch the last few years."

I gave her a wry smile. "I know that too."

Tears shimmered on her lashes. "But I love her. I don't want to lose her, Nick."

I cupped her face, pressing kisses to her cheeks, capturing her tears with my lips. "You won't. She'll have the best care. The best doctors. Whatever she needs. I swear it."

"But what if—"

"Shh." I pulled her into my chest, holding her tight. "The unknown will remain so until we land. There's little point entertaining the possibilities."

"What do I do if not worry?"

I cast around, looking for any distraction available as the plane began to taxi.

"Tell me about our life."

"What?"

"Our future, Collins. Tell me about the future we'll have together."

Her lip wobbled. "You really want to know?"

"I do. More than anything."

She considered me for a minute, then nodded. "There will be kids."

"Of course."

"A whole household. Enough for a soccer team."

"Noted."

"And a dog. One that likes to get muddy."

I raised an eyebrow. "A big one?"

She shrugged, her shoulders relaxing as the plane became airborne. "I don't mind."

"Great, I'll be in charge of dog adopting then."

"We'll holiday at the beach. And show them the world."

"Agreed."

"And you'll teach them how to make gnocchi."

"So long as you teach them your super secret waffle recipe."

We exchanged a smile.

"And there will be love. So much love we'll have to get married all over again just to celebrate it."

I pulled her close, pressing a kiss to her ring finger. "If I could, I'd marry you every year. Every month. Every day."

She closed her eyes, dropping her head to my shoulder. "I love you."

"I love you too, *Tesoro*. Now, tell me. Will there be date nights in this future? Because I think we're going to need Emily and Calvin to babysit our team of children."

She tilted her head back, her expression grateful. "Of course, Calvin and Emily will babysit. Every single time we ask."

"Perfect."

~

"Come on," I whispered to an exhausted Collins. "Let's leave them alone."

"But—"

I tugged her hand. "They need time to process, *Tesoro*."

She glanced back at her sister and brother-in-law, both of them looking lost and overwhelmed.

With a reluctant gait, she followed me from the room, leaving the husband and wife alone.

We'd been here for two days—two long, tiring, emotionally exhausting days.

"Amnesia," Collins muttered, shaking her head. "I can't believe it."

"They said her memory might come back."

"Mmm."

I hesitated in the hall, unsure of where to go.

"Nick?"

"*Tesoro?*"

She wrapped her arms around me, pressing her face to my chest. "Thank you. For being here. For holding me. For... everything."

I held her tight, keeping my arms around her. "Of course. I love you. There's nowhere I'd rather be."

She tilted her head back, offering me a tired but gorgeous smile. "Nowhere?"

I laughed, kissing her smiling lips. "Well, maybe one place."

"Does it start with a b and end with a d and have a vowel in between?"

"You read my mind."

With a grin, she squeezed my waist. "Then let's go find a bed, husband."

And after a long nap, I slid inside her, my cock burying deep as her pussy clenched tightly around me.

"Here," I whispered against her ear as I made love to my wife. "Here with you is where I'd rather be every single second of every single day forever."

With a cry, Collins came, her teeth sinking into my shoulder, my control breaking at the bite of pain.

"Voglio fare l'amore con te ogni giorno della nostra vita. Voglio toccarti come il tesoro che sei. Voglio adorare la tua fica con la stessa adorazione che un discepolo ha per un dio. Sei mio, Collins. E sarò per sempre tuo, il mio cuore," I groaned, fucking into her roughly as I came, my cock milked by her glorious cunt.

"Love you," I whispered as we both panted, our bodies still thrumming with desire. "I love you so fucking much."

"Forever," Collins said, her expression fierce.

"Forever and a day," I promised.

EPILOGUE ONE

Collins

I finished signing the fifth and final stack of papers, double-checking the date before handing the pen back to our accountant. He checked it over, then gave one short, sharp nod.

"This looks good. I'll lodge the forms today, and we can get this sorted within the week."

"Thanks, Alistair." I stood, pressing a hand to the back of the small baby strapped to my chest. "If there's nothing else, we might go meet daddy, hey Leo?" I asked the sleeping bundle on my chest.

The baby didn't answer, but that didn't concern me. A deep well of contentment had settled in my soul from the moment the nurses had placed Leo in my arms.

Two years had passed since I'd enacted what we now laughingly termed the 'Mrs. Clause'. Two years of laughter and tears, love, and fears.

Two years of infertility.

After the first six months, we'd undergone some testing only to be told it was unlikely we'd ever naturally conceive. Despite the heartache that had come, we'd been determined to start a family that comprised of more than just the two of us.

After months of adoption papers, house assessments, and a few missed opportunities, we'd received the phone call.

"Mrs. Del Laurentis?"

"Yes?" I'd asked, pressing the phone between my shoulder and my ear as I dusted my hands on my apron. "Can I help you?"

"Mrs. Del Laurentis, this is Vivian from Little Miracles Adoptions. I'm calling because we have a mother who would like us to discuss an adoption with you."

I froze my body on high alert. "I'm—I'm sorry. Can you repeat that?"

Vivian's voice was warm and supportive. "The mother chose you and Mr. Del Laurentis from the applicant list. The baby was born yesterday, and the mother would like us to discuss an adoption with you today. Are you still interested?"

We'd met Leo later that afternoon and took

him home later that week. For a month, we'd been on tenterhooks, falling in love with our baby but knowing that his biological mother had thirty days to change her mind. Instead, she'd only asked one thing of us—that we send updates about Leo every year via the adoption agency.

I didn't know her name; I didn't know anything beyond the barest of details about her medical history and Leo's birth. But I prayed for her every day and had made a promise to myself that I would send her letters every month for the rest of my life to thank her for the gift she bestowed upon us. Leo would never know anything but love from us.

To ensure we could always take care of our son, Nick had immediately set up a trust fund. Even if the world collapsed on our business, Leo's future would be secure.

I found Nick sitting at a table in the café in the lobby of the accounting building.

"Hey," I said, settling at the table. "Have you ordered for me?"

"Just a coffee." He slid a menu across to me with a wink. "And because I know you like to find the most chocolatey thing on the menu and refuse to order it, so I've already got two coming."

I glanced down, laughing as I realised he

was pointing at the chocolate fudge waffles. "Sounds perfect, actually."

The small bundle tightly strapped to my chest made a small wet sound. A familiar smell immediately followed.

"Here, I got him." Nick bent, scooping up the strap of the diaper bag and throwing it over his shoulder before holding out his hands for Leo. I transferred him and watched, heart expanding, as my two boys headed off to the bathroom, Nick muttering about how impressed he was with Leo's ability to produce gag-worthy smells.

Those boys are going to be trouble.

"Here you go, hun." The waitress arrived, sliding the two plates onto the table. "You need anything else?"

I glanced at Nick's cup and ordered another coffee. We weren't getting a lot of sleep with the little one at the moment.

"Gotcha." She made a note on her pad. "Just gotta say, it's nice to see he finally made a move." She winked at me. "Looks like it paid off too."

I tilted my head, giving her a small confused smile. "Sorry?"

She nodded toward the bathrooms. "That guy? You're married, right?"

I nodded, mystified by the direction of this conversation.

"I've owned this place for twenty years. I

know all my regulars, know all the ones to keep an eye on. He's been coming in here for the better part of a decade. Cool guy big tipper. Doesn't come in very often, but does it enough that I pay attention. Every year he'd come in, sit down at this table and watch you." She grinned. "Nice to know he finally manned up and asked you out. Looks like it paid off for him too, what with you being his wife and that little bubba you got now." She tapped her pen against her notepad. "I'll bring you that coffee."

I watched her walk away, a suspicious feeling niggling in my gut. I reached for my phone, dialling Alistair.

"Collins? Did we forget something?"

"I just had one question. In the last five years, did Nick come to the firm to do his paper-work, or did you ship it to London?"

"Here. He always came to the office. Actu-ally, he always came and finished about an hour before you."

"Thanks, Alistair."

"Is there a reason you—?"

"No," I interrupted, that warm gooey love feeling spreading. "But thank you."

"Sure, anytime." The man sounded con-fused, but I didn't care. This would be my little secret.

Nick returned to the table; Leo's tiny body

cradled against his shoulder. "Our son is clean and smelling daisy fresh. At least for the next five minutes," Nick declared, sitting down.

I grinned, not even caring if I looked like a fool.

"What?" he asked, dropping the bag on the ground, his big hand holding Leo steady.

"I love you." I pushed everything I was feeling at that moment into the declaration.

His eyebrows raised in surprise, but he grinned his gaze warming. "Love you too, Co."

He glanced down at his plate, his eyes narrowing. "Wait. Is this because you stole a piece of my waffle?"

I threw back my head and laughed.

EPILOGUE TWO

Nick

I stood barefoot on the beach; the waters lapping quietly behind me as I shifted in place. Down the makeshift aisle, the late afternoon sun at her back, walked Collins. Her boho lace dress brushed the sand as she glided toward me, her gaze firmly fixed on mine.

The select audience consisted of Collins' sister, Emily, her husband, Calvin, their two children; and Collins' friends Ella, Blue, Anika and Honey and their families.

And, of course, our three gorgeous children—who were shockingly silent as they watched their mother walk toward me. The silence was a miraculous occurrence considering all five children were under the age of ten.

"Mommy, you look beautiful!" Our second youngest, Bonny, yelled, shattering the awed silence.

So much for a miracle.

My beautiful wife paused to send the kids a wink. Emily and Calvin whispered something to the children, and they immediately dove for the bubbles, blowing them with gusto toward the aisle.

The photographer shifted in the background, finger rapidly clicking to capture Collins, her hair tossed, her curls spiralling down her back as she laughed into the cloud of bubbles engulfing her.

The solo acoustic guitarist strummed, singing Noah Reid's version of *'Simply the Best'* as Collins resumed her walk. Emily and Calvin kept the assembled children as contained as possible as Collins reached me, slipping her hands into mine.

"You look beautiful, *Tesoro*."

She smiled, the happiness I felt reflected on her face. "Thanks. You look pretty amazing yourself, husband."

The celebrant cleared his throat. "Dearly beloved, we are gathered here today—"

Much like our first wedding, I barely paid attention to the words coming from the man before me. All my attention was centred on my wife. I'd surprised her with the idea, and she'd passionately agreed to renew our vows.

And the wedding night—

"The bride and groom have decided to write their own vows. I now invite Nicholas to speak."

I cleared my throat, joy choking me. "Collins, when we first entered this marriage, we were little more than children. We swore to love and protect each other, naïve and unaware of the road we would need to travel. But here we are, together, in love."

I looked over at our children, Leo wrinkling his nose at us, Bonny swishing her dress from side to side, and our youngest, Jesse, watching us with his solemn expression. None of these children were of my blood, but all had my heart.

"We're parents now. And I couldn't ask for a better way to spend today than having our children witness this moment." I looked back at her, falling in love again with her smile, her eyes, the radiant happiness shining from her soul. "You are my heart. You are my soul. And I will forever be grateful for every moment of this life we share together. I love you, *Tesoro*. Thank you for making my life beautiful."

She swiped a tear away as the children applauded behind us, Calvin and Emily gently shushing them, allowing space for Collins to speak.

"Nicholas, years ago, I walked away because I thought you didn't love me. I forced our reunion because I was determined to fill my life with love. The love of a family—even if that family was only a baby and me."

She brushed a hand over her cheek, wiping away tears. "I could have never predicted that moment would result in us finding our way back. I could never have predicted the joy our beautiful children have brought to our life every day." She drew in a shaky breath, her lips wobbling. "You are my heart. You own my soul. Every day I am grateful for your demands when I asked that first question. Your doggedness delivered us to this life together. Thank you for this incredible journey we're on. Every day I choose you and this life we live. Thank you for loving me."

The children clapped, their exuberance turning to sounds of dismay as I drew their mother close, pressing hot kisses to her mouth.

"Ew!" I heard Leo protest. "They're kissing. Again!"

"My mommy and daddy do the same," Leo's cousin Josie informed him.

"But they do it all the time," Jesse complained, his little boy voice sounding very put out.

"Mommy says kissing is what people who are in love do," our Bonny explained.

I drew back, brushing a thumb over Collins' precious cheek. She gazed up at me, love written in every line of her beautiful face.

Yeah, this is exactly what people in love do.

And for the rest of my life, I'd be thanking the Gods, Santa, or perhaps the lawyer who'd drafted the clause in tour prenup that was re-sponsible for bringing my wife back to me.

"I love you, wife. Forever."

She smiled. "Forever and a day, husband. I love you, Nick. Thanks for being the best-arranged marriage I've ever had."

I hope you loved Collins and Nick. Honestly, these two made me swoon more than any other book I've written! I LOVED THEM! Be sure to check out the bonus slice of life on my website.

You can also read the entire series by checking them out on my website at
www.EvieMitchell.com

*If you enter the code **EBOOK10** you can get 10% off your purchase from my website.*

THE MRS. CLAUSE
TRANSLATIONS

Cuore mio—my heart

Nemmeno immagini cosa ho intenzione di farti—You can't even imagine what I'm going to do to you

Tesoro—Treasure or honey

Amo il tuo sapore, Tesoro—I love your taste, honey

Giusto, Tesoro?—Right, honey?

Grazie per avermi restituito il mio cuore. Senza di te, il mio petto era una cavità vuota, la mia vita senza luce o speranza. Sei la mia anima, Collins. Il mio tutto—Thank you for giving me my heart back. Without you, my chest was an empty cavity, my life without light or hope. You are my soul, Collins. My everything.

Voglio fare l'amore con te ogni giorno della nostra vita. Voglio toccarti come il tesoro che sei.

Voglio adorare la tua fica con la stessa adorazione che un discepolo ha per un dio. Sei mio, Collins. E sarò per sempre tuo, il mio cuore—I want to make love to you every day of our lives. I want to touch you like the treasure you are. I want to worship your cunt with the same adoration a disciple has for a god. You are mine, Collins. And I will forever be yours, my heart.

ABOUT THE AUTHOR

Evie Mitchell is a thirty-something romance author (she/her/hers) living with disability. She believes in inclusion, accessibility, and fierce romance. Her loves include steamy romance novels, her husband, their THREE sausage dogs (heaven help her), and her ever-growing collection of book-related mugs.

As a woman with a diverse work history including in areas such as emergency response, event management, human rights, disability access, and security - her books are filled with true stories (bridezillas), worst-case scenarios (malfunctioning dresses), and her favorite tropes (one-bed).

Evie specialises in fiercely inclusive happily ever afters.

ALSO BY EVIE MITCHELL

Capricorn Cove Series

The Shake-Up

Double the D

Muffin Top

The Mrs. Clause

New Year Knew You

Double Breasted

As You Wish

You Sleigh Me

Resolution Revolution

Meat Load

Larsson Siblings Series

Thunder Thighs

Clean Sweep

The X-list

Reality Check

The Christmas Contract

Dogg Pack Books

Puppy Love

<u>Bad English</u>

<u>The Frock Up</u>

<u>Pier Pressure</u>

All Access Series

Knot My Type

Love Flushed

Nameless Souls MC Series

<u>Runner</u>

<u>Wrath</u>

<u>Ghost</u>

<u>Shield</u>

Elliot Security Series

<u>Rough Edge</u>

<u>Bleeding Edge</u>

www.ingramcontent.com/pod-product-compliance
Lightning Source LLC
Chambersburg PA
CBHW010438170726
48283CB00011B/3274